THREE CHEERS FOR KEISHA
by Teresa Reed

Illustrations by
Eric Velasquez

Spot Illustrations by
Rich Grote

MAGIC ATTIC PRESS

Published by Magic Attic Press.

For more information contact:
Book Editor, Magic Attic Press, 866 Spring Street,
P.O. Box 9712, Portland, ME 04104-9954.

First Edition
Printed in the United States of America
1 2 3 4 5 6 7 8 9 10

Betsy Gould, Editorial Director
Marva Martin, Art Director
Robin Haywood, Managing Editor

Edited by Judit Bodnar
Designed by Susi Oberhelman

Library of Congress Cataloging-in-Publications Data

ISBN: 1-57513-008-4

CIP 95-77944

As members of the
MAGIC ATTIC CLUB,
we promise to
be best friends,
share all of our adventures in the attic,
use our imaginations,
have lots of fun together,
and remember—the real magic is in us.

Alison   Keisha

Heather   Megan

Table of Contents

KEISHA'S BIG DREAM

ood afternoon, ladies and gentlemen. This is your principal, Mr. Roberts." Keisha Vance stopped working on her math problems and glanced up at the classroom loudspeaker.

"This year," the principal's voice continued, "Lincoln School will have official cheerleaders for all sporting events. Anyone who is interested in trying out should see Ms. Henderson immediately after school today to get further information and permission slips. Tryouts will be held in the gym next Monday at three-thirty."

When the final bell rang,
Keisha tapped her best friend,
Heather Hardin, on the shoulder.
"This is really great! We've never
had a cheerleading squad before,"
she said, adjusting the barrette
that held her dark brown hair in

place. "But we've only got one week to get
ready!" Keisha had wanted to be a cheerleader ever since
she could remember, and she planned to try out for a
squad when she got to high school. She never imagined
she'd get her chance so soon!

"I know!" said Heather. "But I don't know if I should try
out for it. I've already got dance lessons twice a week."
Heather stood up from her desk and tried to stand on
pointe in her pink sneakers.

"Oh, don't worry about that right now," said Keisha,
grinning at Heather's attempt. "Let's get Alison and
Megan and go see Ms. Henderson right away."

"Keisha, did you hear the announcement?" Alison
McCann asked when Keisha and Heather ran up to her at
the fifth-grade lockers. Alison was wearing her favorite
blue jumpsuit.

Megan Ryder finished putting her books in her locker

and turned to her friends. "Are you going to try out for the squad?"

"Well—" Heather began.

"I sure am!" Keisha answered. "We'd better hurry before the permission slips are all gone."

At the entrance to the gym, Ms. Henderson was surrounded by thirty or so girls and boys. "I didn't think so many people would want to be on the squad," said Megan.

"Oh, I think it's exciting," said Heather.

"Even more exciting than the Magic Attic Club?" asked Alison, winking at Heather. When their neighbor, Ellie Goodwin, had moved back into town last winter, she'd invited them to play in her attic. The four friends had found an old trunk filled with beautiful costumes. And when they'd tried on outfits and stood in front of the mirror, they'd found themselves on an unexpected adventure. They had formed the Magic Attic Club, and now they were closer than ever before.

"Alison, you know that's not what I mean," said Heather. She put her hands on her hips in mock exasperation.

"Come on, you guys," said Keisha, laughing and gently pushing her friends through the throng.

As the girls waited for their permission slips, Keisha

examined a poster of a cheerleader that was tacked up on the gym bulletin board. I'm going to be the most incredible cheerleader ever, she thought. I can see myself leading a whole routine! My dad says I'm a natural.

"Keisha, what kinds of stunts do you think we're going to have to do for the tryout?" Heather asked on the way home.

"Oh, probably cartwheels and flips and handsprings, the kinds of things I'm learning in gymnastics. Don't worry, once we make the squad, we can all practice together."

Megan quickly turned toward Keisha. "Well, I don't really . . ."

"We are going to have so much fun," said Keisha, grasping Megan's hand. "I just know it! Oh, and Alison, you'll love cheerleading because you're so athletic."

"But. . ." Alison tried to interrupt Keisha.

"And Heather," Keisha continued, "you'll be really good at it, too. I watch the cheerleading routines whenever my dad takes me to a basketball game, and it's a lot like a ballet—every move is choreographed."

As the girls walked along, Keisha chattered on. She was so excited, she didn't notice how quiet Alison, Heather, and Megan had become. When they reached Keisha's house, she turned and waved goodbye to her

Cheerleader
Squad

friends and ran up the flower-bordered walkway to her front door.

"Mama, I'm so glad you're here," she said, giving her mother an extra big hug. Her mother was a nurse at the local hospital and her father was the hospital administrator. They sometimes worked long hours, and Keisha didn't always get to see them when she came home from school. "Guess what? They're starting a cheerleading squad at school and you've got to sign my permission slip!"

"Really? Now aren't you glad you took all those gymnastics classes?" It was clear that Keisha got her height and slimness from her mother, who bent down to hug Keisha and give her a kiss on the cheek. "I bet knowing how to do tricks like handsprings and roundoffs will be a big help. So will all that work on timing and precision. I always knew my Keisha-girl's dreams would come true. Come into the kitchen and tell me all about it."

While Keisha talked to her mom, she played a game of I *Spy* with her five-year-old sister, Ashley. Her brother, Ronnie, napped in his portable sleeper nearby.

After dinner Keisha went upstairs to finish her homework. In a while her mom called up to her from the bottom of the stairs. "Keisha, honey, have you decided what you want for dessert Saturday night?"

Saturday! How could she have forgotten about her very first Magic Attic Club sleepover party? She was thrilled when her mom had said okay to having the party. They had sat down together and planned what time her friends should arrive on Saturday and what they would eat, but Keisha needed to figure out what she and the girls would do at the party and what to serve for dessert.

"Sorry, Mom," Keisha answered, going to the head of the stairs. "I'll think about it tonight and let you know first thing tomorrow."

"Okay, honey, we'll talk in the morning."

Keisha finished her homework as quickly as possible, but it wasn't easy to concentrate with the party and the tryouts on her mind. Suddenly she jumped up from her desk and twirled around the room. I'll make up a cheerleading routine for the girls to try at my party, she thought. There are lots of movements they already know from gym class and ballet. Once they see how much fun it is, they'll definitely want to become cheerleaders.

That night Keisha went to sleep imagining herself tumbling around the school gym without stopping. When she did a back flip to the top of a human pyramid, the audience gasped and applauded her amazing athletic skill.

The week flew by and before Keisha knew it, Saturday had arrived. She got up extra early and had almost finished straightening her room when her mother knocked on the door.

"Good morning, baby," she said with a big smile. "Are you ready to go? You know there's always a long line at the market on Saturdays."

Keisha hurried downstairs, where her father was sitting at the kitchen table with Ronnie and Ashley. Keisha couldn't help but giggle as she buttered a muffin. There seemed to be more scrambled egg on her father's Howard University sweatshirt than on her two-year-old brother's plate.

"Tonight's the night, eh, Pumpkin," said Mr. Vance, nodding at Keisha as he struggled to get a spoon into Ronnie's mouth. "Your big party."

Even though Ronnie was only a baby, Keisha couldn't get over how much her father and her brother looked alike. They both had husky builds, with round brown faces, and very curly light brown hair.

"Can I go to the party, too?" asked Ashley. Her long, dark hair was braided into dozens of tiny little braids. Today Mom had fixed them with small yellow beads to match her outfit.

"Sorry, Ash, you're too little. This party's just for me

and my friends." A little look of disappointment came over Ashley's face. Keisha bent over to give her sister a peck on the cheek and quickly added, "But next weekend you and I will play together as much as you want."

On the drive to the supermarket, Keisha described the cheerleading game to her mother.

"Well, honey, it sounds like fun," said Mrs. Vance as she pulled into the parking lot and turned off the car engine, "but everyone might not want to play. Why don't you plan something else, just in case?"

"But, Mom, these are my very best friends. We do everything together. We ride our bikes together and do our homework together," Keisha exclaimed. "Besides, it's my party."

"Keisha," her mother said gently, "just because it's your party, it doesn't mean that everyone will want to do what you want."

"You'll see," Keisha said decisively. "Everyone is going to have fun at my party, and they'll love the game so much that we'll all end up trying out for the cheerleading squad together."

Two

PARTY BLUES

K eisha's doorbell rang at exactly six-thirty that evening. "Hi, Megan! I knew it would be you," said Keisha, taking Megan's yellow jacket and hanging it in the front hall closet. Megan grinned as she handed Keisha her cap and shook out her hair.

"You're the only one of us who's always on time," Keisha told her. Then she set Megan's little flowered suitcase by the closet.

"I almost came over this morning, but I held out as

long as I could," Megan laughed. She loved spending time at Keisha's house. There was always so much going on. Sometimes she wished she had a brother or sister. Ronnie and Ashley were so cute, and they obviously adored their big sister.

"Here, Keisha, I brought that cool new board game that all the older kids are playing," said Megan. "Would you believe it arrived in the mail from my father a couple of days ago? I was keeping it as a surprise for tonight."

"Thanks, Megan, but I've planned something else for us to do." Before Megan could say anything else, the bell rang again. When Keisha opened the door, Heather and Alison stood on the front steps. They were surrounded by duffel bags, sleeping bags, and a couple of shopping bags filled with favorite pillows and stuffed animals.

"Hey, come on in, you two." Keisha pulled her friends and their bags inside.

"Hello, girls," said Keisha's parents, coming out to greet her friends.

As Ashley stood behind her father and said a shy hello, Ronnie boldly ran around in circles in front of everyone. He couldn't put whole sentences together yet, but that didn't stop him from making sure people got to know him.

Keisha's parents told everyone to help themselves to

the food in the kitchen. Then her dad began waving Ashley's and Ronnie's favorite storybooks above his head to entice them back into the family room and away from Keisha and her friends.

When Keisha showed the girls the table she and her mom had set, they squealed with delight. A beautiful blue-and-white, tie-dyed runner ran down the middle of the massive oak table. Each of the four place settings had a placemat and napkin that matched the runner. In the middle of each plate was a small box made of pale woven straw with a blue ribbon tied around it in a bow.

"Where did you find these?" gasped Megan, picking up the box.

"My mom got them at an African flea market," said Keisha proudly. "They're traditional African gifts that are given when you welcome special friends to your home."

"Oh, Keisha," said Heather, who had already taken the lid off of her box. "It's perfect for all my little earrings and rings. Thank you!"

"Thanks, Keisha," said Alison, "I know just where I'm going to put this in my room. I'll use it for my bead collection."

Mrs. Vance had made Keisha's favorite dinner of fried chicken and corn muffins stuffed with pieces of baked apple. There was a big bowl of macaroni salad with chopped red and green peppers and little bits of cooked yellow squash in it, so that it looked like confetti. The girls ate until they thought they would burst.

When they'd cleared off the table, Keisha's mom appeared in the doorway.

"That's the tallest cake I've ever seen!" exclaimed Megan.

"It's a seven-layer sweet potato pecan cake!" said Keisha. "It's my favorite and my grandmother's favorite, too. Grandma and Mom made it special for us tonight." Keisha gave her mother a great big smile and then picked up a stack of dessert plates.

When everyone finished their cake, Keisha called out, "Okay, everybody up to my room. I have a special surprise to show you."

"Shouldn't we help clean up?" asked Megan.

"Don't worry about the kitchen," said Mrs. Vance. "You're at a party. Just go and enjoy yourselves. Keisha's father and I will do the dishes later."

The girls went out into the hallway and grabbed their bags. Then they followed Keisha up the stairs to her room.

"Wow! It looks like you've added twenty new pictures since the last time I was here," said Heather, walking over to a wall that Keisha had covered with photographs.

Besides gymnastics and cheerleading, Keisha loved photography. Her father had bought her first camera for her when she was only six years old. Ever since then Keisha took pictures every chance she got.

"Look!" cried Alison, following Heather over to the wall. "There's Megan and me at the Winter Carnival. You must have taken this picture right before the big snowball fight. All I remember from that night is getting soaked!"

"Why don't you take our picture right now?" asked Alison, striking a silly pose.

"Good idea, Keish," said Heather, and she began twirling around.

"I'm ready for my close-up, Mr. DeMille," said Megan, framing her face with her hands.

"Well, I was just about to show you my surprise. I do *happen* to have one of my cameras right here, though," Keisha said with a grin. "But let's go down to the living room. I don't have any photos of you there, and the light's better. My flash is out for repairs."

The girls trooped back downstairs.

"Now I have to load the film. This is a brand-new camera from my dad," Keisha explained, "and I'm just learning how to use it. . . . Okay . . . there, I'm ready. . . . Now everyone get into a funny pose.

"Get closer together. Now when I count to three, yell PIZZA!" Keisha snapped one picture and then took two more just to make sure she had the right camera settings and in case something went wrong when the film was being developed.

"Now, Ali, why don't you take some pictures? Here, take one of me doing a high kick like this one. And you can take some of me doing a drop-down and a pop-up. First I drop to the floor like this." Keisha squatted and rested on her heels while Alison worked the camera.

"Then for the pop-up, you just jump up in the air as high as you can." The shutter clicked several times as Keisha jumped with her arms outstretched over her head.

"Now you can take a picture of—"

"Keisha, my eyes are crossing. Can we stop now?" cried Alison.

Even Megan sounded a little irritable. "Enough pictures, okay, Keisha?"

"Well, okay. How did you like the routine? Do any of you want to try it?"

"Oh, Keisha, I don't feel like jumping around now," said Alison. "Can't we learn the routine tomorrow?"

"You know, my mom gave me this videotape of Little Women for my birthday," said Heather, pulling a videocassette out of a pocket in her duffel bag. "I was hoping you guys would want to watch it together."

"And look what I have," said Megan, rattling the board game over her head. "My father just sent it to me from Japan. He said it's super popular over there, too"

"Oh wow!" Heather and Alison exclaimed as they rushed over to Megan.

"Mark has one but he won't let me go near it," said Alison.

"Jenna asked Mom to buy this for us," said Heather, "but all the stores are sold out. I can't believe you have it."

As Keisha watched her friends' growing excitement over Megan's game, she began to feel a little hurt. After all, she had worked really hard on her routine. "Come on, I'll show you all how to do the first steps. They're very easy."

"We're stuffed. Let's play one round of the game first, Keisha," Megan pleaded.

"Let's. After that, maybe we'll be ready for you to teach us the routine. Okay, Keisha?" said Heather, sounding as diplomatic as she could.

"Count me out on the cheerleading tonight," said Alison. "I've eaten so much I think even my teeth are full!" She slumped to the floor with a loud thump and a giggle.

"If you'd rather play that game than learn my cheerleading routine, fine," Keisha said, sounding a little more angry than she meant to.

"Keisha, why are you so upset?" asked Heather.

"I've been waiting all week to show you this routine. I worked hard on it!" explained Keisha.

"I want to learn it, just not now," Alison said firmly.

"Okay! We'll play the game!" Keisha sat down next to Megan, who quietly tore the wrapper off the box. All Keisha had wanted to do was share her favorite thing with her friends, but when she looked up and saw their faces, she remembered what her mother had said that morning.

Chapter
Three

MIXED
FEELINGS

On Monday morning Keisha was the first to arrive at school and search for her friends. Finally Heather came down the hall.

"Morning, Heather," Keisha said softly to her best friend when she reached her locker. "Hey, you know I think you left one of your barrettes under my bed. I'll bring it in for you tomorrow."

"Thanks," said Heather, and quickly busied herself by looking through her book bag.

Soon Alison and Megan joined them.

"Hi, Ali. Hi, Megan," Keisha said, hoping to sound as cheerful as possible. "Listen, I'm sorry about Saturday night," "It's just—"

"Don't worry about it, Keisha," said Alison. "We understand."

"You do? So we'll all meet later?"

"Sorry, Keisha, but I've really got to work on my skating routine," said Alison.

"I have a dance lesson at three-thirty." said Heather.

"My piano lesson with Ellie is right after school," said Megan. "But good luck today, Keish."

Keisha spent the rest of the morning thinking of a way to get her friends more interested in cheerleading. When the lunch bell rang, she ran to sit at the table she and her Magic Attic Club friends shared.

"Hi, guys. What's up?" Keisha asked.

Alison and Megan nodded and Heather's "Hello" sounded unusually soft.

"I know that you can't make the tryouts today," said Keisha, "but maybe Ms. Henderson will let you try out tomorrow or something."

Megan and Alison exchanged glances.

25

"You know, you're so good at all those moves that gymnasts make, I think cheerleading is perfect for you," said Megan. "But I really don't think it's for me."

"Once you practiced the tumbling, you'd get the hang of it in no time. Besides, I thought that since we're best friends, we'd all try out for the squad together."

"We might not all make it anyhow," said Heather.

Alison gave Keisha a reassuring smile. "Besides, you're great at everything you do. You'll be fine."

Heather and Megan quickly nodded in agreement.

"I'll try to make as many of the squad games as I can," said Megan.

"You know I'd go with you if I could," said Heather.

"I know, Heather."

Then Megan started explaining the plot of a mystery book she was reading. Keisha tried to hide her hurt feelings and listen, but she couldn't get her mind off the tryouts.

At three o'clock Keisha bolted out of her seat and ran to her locker. She was a little nervous, especially without her best friends. Once she had changed into her leotard and shorts, she felt better. She entered the gym and made her way through the crowd.

Wow! she thought. There must be dozens of kids here. I'm going to have to perform perfectly if I'm going to make the squad.

Mixed Feelings

Ms. Henderson was talking to a student aide who had come to help her with the music. A few parents were scattered throughout the bleachers. I wish Mom didn't have to work today, thought Keisha. She shrugged off her disappointment and went over her routine again in her mind. I really want to make the squad and I've got to do my best whether Mom and my friends are here or not.

"All right, people!" Ms. Henderson's voice boomed. "Let's line up in two groups by height."

Keisha quickly joined a line. Her palms were damp as she looked around at the others. She really hadn't expected so many kids to show up at the tryouts.

"First, we're going to do some warm-ups. Then I want you to form a line, make a running start and end with a somersault on the mat here in front of me. Let's go!"

The contestants did jumping jacks and paired off to do stretching exercises. Then Ms. Henderson began the tumbling routine. When Keisha's turn came she took a running jump and somersaulted effortlessly on the mat.

"Very good, everyone! Now I want you to pick up a set of pom-pons and make a large circle around the gym. When I tap you on the shoulder, break the circle and do a high kick and a split V kick in the middle of the circle. I want each of you to go as high as you can on the split V."

The longer the tryouts lasted, the more excited Keisha

became. When Ms. Henderson tapped her, she ran out and did the highest kick and split she'd ever done.

"Now everyone take a seat," said Ms. Henderson. "How many of you have made up a routine for today?"

Most of the group raised their hands.

"Good. I want the people who have routines in one group and the ones who don't in another."

Ms. Henderson's glasses slid down her nose while she surveyed the group. "Maybe some of you who don't have a routine will think of something while you watch the others. And remember, we have a lot of people here today, so I'm going to give each of you just three minutes."

When Keisha gathered up her pom-pons and began her routine, she suddenly remembered what her gymnastics coach had drilled into her. She flashed her biggest, brightest smile. Then she began,

We've got the Spirit! We've got the Team!
Defense, Defense! You're Supreme!

Keisha finished her routine with a handspring, then did a split on the floor. A second went by and she heard a few people applaud. Keisha was sure she saw the corners of Ms. Henderson's mouth turn up in a tiny smile.

Chapter
Four

A NATURAL LEADER

K eisha felt fantastic. She knew that
Ms. Henderson was going to
consider her for the team. She just knew it!
On the walk home, she wished her friends
were around so she could talk about the tryouts.

As she turned up her walkway, she glanced down the
street. There was Ellie Goodwin, arranging several pots of
flowers on her front porch. Suddenly Keisha wanted to
talk to Ellie and visit her attic more than anything in the

world. She raced into the house, dropped her books on the hall table, and shouted, "Mom, I'm going to Ellie's."

"Keisha dear," Ellie said when she opened the front door. "You look like you've had quite a day. Care to come in and tell me about it?"

"I think this is one of the best and worst days of my entire life," Keisha said as she followed Ellie inside.

"I've had days like that myself," said Ellie comfortingly. "Tell me everything."

Almost in one big breath, Keisha told Ellie about going out for the cheerleading squad, and about the party and how no one could try out with her.

Ellie gave her a big hug. "I'm sure you'll work everything out, Keisha," she said.

Keisha glanced toward the entryway. "Would it be okay to go up to the attic for a while?"

"Why, of course, dear." Ellie patted Keisha's shoulder. "You go right ahead."

Keisha took the key from the silver box in the front hall and walked up the stairs. She unlocked the attic door and climbed the next flight. It was the first time she had been up there without her friends, and it felt very strange. She stood for a moment and glanced around at the letters, figurines, and other treasures that Ellie had collected during her travels around the world.

Then Keisha squared her shoulders and crossed the room. Rummaging through the big steamer trunk brought back memories of her first adventure in the attic, especially when she touched the dresses she and her three friends had tried on that day. She hadn't known what to expect that time, either.

Keisha picked up a fancy, pale evening gown with a matching shawl. She threw the shawl around her shoulders, then returned it and the gown to the trunk. She held up a few other outfits, but she just didn't feel like trying them today.

She was getting ready to close the trunk when a purple sweater and matching pleated skirt caught her eye. She pulled them through the tangle of clothes. It was a cheerleading uniform! Digging further, she found sneakers, gold pom-pons, and a megaphone that completed the outfit. Keisha quickly changed clothes.

She ran to the mirror, threw some high kicks in the air, and began to chant, "We've got the spirit! We've got the team! Defense, defense! You're supreme!" She closed her eyes so she could picture each movement of her routine. When she spun around she felt a little light-headed and opened her eyes to steady herself.

Instead of seeing her reflection in the mirror, Keisha

found herself in the middle of an outdoor stadium. Not only was the mirror no longer in front of her, there were about sixty girls staring back at her. They were all smiling and clapping along with her cheer.

"Thank you, Keisha," called a teenager with round-rimmed glasses. "That was a great way to start our morning. We'll take a ten-minute break."

Keisha couldn't believe her eyes. Here she was on a beautiful bright spring day surrounded by other girls in cheerleading outfits! Girls were wandering around the field doing stretches or just talking quietly among themselves. But what exactly was she doing here? And where was here?

"Keisha, that was fantastic!" said an older girl with an "O" on her sweatshirt. "I think you're one of the best cheerleaders we have here today. Is this your first time at cheerleading camp? Oh, by the way, my name's Maggie. Maggie Birchwood."

"Yes. . . . Yes, it's my first time," Keisha answered hesitantly. "What about you, Maggie? You sound like you've done this before."

"Oh, this is my third year," Maggie answered brightly. "Hey, let's do some warm-ups while we wait for Shannon to start up again."

"Who's Shannon?" Keisha asked, still feeling lost.

"Shannon's the head camp instructor, silly! She just told you how great you were. Hey, are you all right? I mean, weren't you at orientation? How could you not know Shannon?"

Before Keisha could answer, Shannon began to speak into her megaphone. "Okay, girls, the instructors have gotten together and decided who today's group leaders will be. We'll have five groups, with fourteen girls in each. As you know, we will assign a new leader every day, so that as many people as possible will have the chance to lead. Mindy Lawrence will be the leader for the Wildcats squad, and Pam Stephens will head up the Panthers. Our choice for the Lions squad is no surprise to any of you . . . It's Keisha Vance."

Chapter
Five

OBSTACLE
COURSE

"Congratulations, Keisha!" said Maggie. "I told you that you were one of the best ones here. I hope I'll be in your group because I have this routine that I want—"

"Excuse me, Maggie," said Shannon, "but I need to speak with Keisha right away." She locked elbows with Keisha and pulled her slightly away from Maggie. "Are you ready to get started?"

Keisha's moment of excitement quickly passed.

"Okay, here's a list of the kids in your squad and a

cheerbook of activities you are to lead them through. We'll break for lunch in an hour and a half. See you then. Good luck!"

Keisha stared at the stack of materials Shannon handed her: a clipboard, a cheerbook, and a binder full of papers and charts. She tried to read, but it was all a blur. I can't lead any classes, Keisha thought. I don't even know if I made my school squad yet!

Shannon watched her for a moment before she spoke. "Are you okay, Keisha? If you're not feeling well, I can assign another leader."

Keisha was about to tell Shannon what she was thinking when a tiny voice spoke in the back of her mind: Don't blow it, Keisha! This is your chance to show everyone what a great cheerleader you really are.

She took a deep breath, looked up at Shannon, and shook her head. "Nothing's wrong."

Shannon smiled. "Great! You can teach the other kids a lot. You're so enthusiastic, and you carry yourself like a pro. Why, you've walked around here with the brightest smile all morning . . . that is, until now."

"I—I'll be fine," Keisha stammered. "I'm just in shock over being chosen as squad leader."

"Look Keisha, everybody's a squad leader for the first time sometime. You'll be okay."

"Thanks," Keisha responded weakly. Well, here goes nothing, she thought, as she adjusted her uniform and walked over to a corner of the field. She blew her whistle and called off the list of names through her megaphone. Soon thirteen girls had assembled in front of her. Keisha was surprised to see how many older girls were in her group.

She was about to start the session when she heard a familiar voice. "Before we start, I was wondering if I could show you a new routine I've just put together."

Keisha looked up from her clipboard. "Well, that's not what we need to do first, Maggie," she answered as calmly as she could.

"But the routine I've worked out is really great, and we might want to use it for our practice sessions." Maggie's look seemed almost to dare Keisha to say no.

Keisha stood her ground. How could Maggie interrupt her when she was busy trying to figure out what to do next? "Not now, Maggie. I've got to run through the cheerbook that Shannon gave me."

Keisha looked over her squad. "Okay, everybody, please form a line so you can hear what we're going to do today." She hoped she made sense. Whenever her class did something outdoors and the teacher wanted them to pay attention, she asked the kids to form a line.

"Okay!" Keisha yelled into the megaphone as loudly as she could. She didn't realize how close she stood to the group—a few of them threw their hands up to their ears and jumped back.

"We always get into a circle when the squad leader has something to tell us," one girl said sweetly.

"Well, okay, good point. Could everyone please gather around me in a circle," said Keisha. As the girls rearranged themselves, she quickly skimmed some of the notes Shannon had given her. "Okay, there will be a competition at the end of the day to see how well each squad has learned the camp routines. Now remember, we're competing against *ourselves* so we can improve our scores on the camp leaders' evaluations. We're here to perfect our own skills, not just to outshine the other squads.

"The first thing on our practice list today is projection." Keisha read aloud from Shannon's notes: "'Projection and spirit are the key elements of every good cheer.' Remember, if the fans can't hear you when you're back at school, you can't get them into your school spirit. And if you don't have school spirit, how can you lead those fans in cheering for a team victory?"

"We have an excellent cheer that we do at my school,"

said Maggie. "It's perfect for learning projection." This time she was almost pleading.

"Thanks, but I have to follow the cheerbook for today's routines. Speaking of projection, though, you did remind me that the way to be loud is to use your diaphragm and not strain your voice." Keisha flipped through the Lion's cheerbook to see which routines to practice for the afternoon, then carefully demonstrated the series of moves. She was amazed to hear herself projecting the cheer clear across the stadium without the megaphone!

Before she was halfway through, another girl spoke out. Her name tag read Darcy Miller. "But can't we make up our own cheers for the exercise? You know, make ours stand out a little."

Keisha thought fast. "Well, Darcy, Shannon was pretty clear about following the cheerbook. Maybe we can work on new cheers tomorrow. Now, who wants to come up here and follow along with me? After that we'll try it as a group." No one moved.

"Come on, it's easy. Who wants to try?"

"I think we should see Maggie's cheer first," said a girl named Tina, who was standing beside Darcy. "Maybe we should show off our own routines and then take a vote to learn the cheer we like best." To Keisha's surprise, the other girls nodded in agreement.

Keisha blew her bangs away from her eyes in frustration. How was she going to whip this team into shape if they wouldn't do what she told them to do? But she didn't think it would help if they knew they were getting to her.

"Let's come back to the projection exercises later," she said, speaking into the megaphone again. She didn't really need the megaphone, but it made her feel on top of the situation. And right now, things seemed very close to spinning out of control.

"Next on our list is practice for the pom-pon routine. When we perform this afternoon, every group has to do the same routine. . . . Oh, and I guess I forgot to mention that the squad that gets the highest scores will have a chance to attend a special intensive workshop on choreography. It will be free for all the winners."

"I still don't understand why we all have to perform the same routines," said Darcy. "I mean, not all of us are good at the same things."

"Well, when we take a break, maybe we can go and talk to Shannon. But right now, we've got to begin our warm-up exercises."

Keisha put down her megaphone and started running in place. She expected everyone to follow along with her. Instead some girls were doing jumping jacks, while others were stretching their legs behind their backs or doing knee bends.

Keisha stopped and spoke into the megaphone. "Why aren't you following me? You should all be doing exactly what I'm doing!"

"But you didn't tell us to do exactly what you're doing," said another girl named Lisa. She sounded almost as frustrated as Keisha felt. "You only said to do some warm-up exercises."

Suddenly Keisha wanted to bolt from the stadium and find her way back home. Maybe cheerleading wasn't for her after all. And where were those natural leadership abilities her father always told her she had?

Chapter

Six

LEADING
THE WAY

Keisha started right in with the next routine. "Okay, we've warmed up enough for now. I'm going to show you how to do the pom-pon routine again and then we'll see if you can pick it up." The girls took a seat on the grass, and Keisha took a pom in each hand.

Out of the corner of her eye, Keisha noticed that some of the girls were sitting a little too far away to hear and see her, but she figured they would join the group once they saw the routine. She decided to ignore them and just concentrate on the activity. Suddenly Keisha realized that she wasn't sure what to do next.

"Okay, guys, just relax for a moment. I need to look over the cheerbook before we get started."

The girls groaned, but Keisha smiled at them and tried to memorize the steps as quickly as possible. When she felt ready, she stood up and saw that a few of the girls had wandered away and were talking to other girls who were on break. She blew her whistle, then called for them to come back and pay attention.

"Okay, now watch," she said, shaking out her pom-pons once the girls had returned to the group. "We're going to repeat this routine to two sets of four counts, so watch carefully."

On the first count Keisha pointed her arms straight out, then clasped the pom-pons together. For the second count she formed a "T" with her right hand out and her left hand on her hip. With the next count Keisha dropped both arms down to her sides. On the final count, she made another "T", this time with her left hand out, and then jumped in the air, pulling her knees up high.

"Do we start with our left or right arm on the second count?" asked a petite girl with freckles and green eyes.

"I'll do it for you again. Now watch closely."

The squad was still struggling with the pom-pon

routine when Shannon appeared. Keisha was so relieved to see her that she asked the girls to rest a moment while she talked to Shannon.

"So, how's it going, Keisha? You seem to be having a little difficulty."

"I think I need a new group of girls," Keisha whispered. "Nothing is going right!"

"Calm down, Keisha," Shannon said soothingly. Then she turned to the group and spoke into her megaphone. "You guys are really lucky. You're getting two breaks in a row. I'll see all of you back here in ten minutes, and there will be no exceptions!" The girls picked up their gear and walked toward the field entrance without so much as one questioning look.

"How did you do that?" Keisha asked incredulously. "Those girls won't do a single thing I say. At first all they wanted to do was show me their routines, and now none of them can seem to pick up the steps for today's routine."

Shannon gave Keisha a sympathetic smile. "Maybe they're not the only ones here to learn something."

"What do you mean?"

"Well, it seems to me you're doing a lot of showing and telling, but the girls aren't getting to do anything."

"You said that I had a lot to show them, and that's exactly what I'm doing."

46

"Have you given them a chance to show you what *they* can do? Do you know what each member of your group does best?"

Keisha stared blankly at Shannon.

"I think you've been trying a little too hard, Keisha. People have to learn things on their own. Why don't you try sharing some of the work with the girls? I think everything will go a lot better."

"You're right," Keisha said after a moment's thought. "Hey, it might even be easier your way," Keisha smiled.

Shannon bopped Keisha lightly on the shoulder and smiled, too. "Why don't you do three laps around the field to clear your head. I'll bring your squad back to you in a few minutes. And when you start again just pretend everything that happened before has been erased."

"Thanks, Shannon."

"Don't worry, it's all going to work out fine. Do the pom-pon routine until we break for lunch. Afterward you'll work on the two-tier pyramid."

"I don't know if we're ready for competition yet—to be evaluated, I mean."

"Keisha, I know your squad can do it—if you can get everyone to work together." Shannon smiled again and walked away.

Shannon's pep talk really hit home. She was glad that Shannon thought her group had what it took to score well on the day's evaluation. Now that she believed it, she had to get the girls to see it, too. As she walked around the edge of the field she thought, Shannon *is* right. People will join in if I let them. With a smile, Keisha broke into a jog.

After several laps she rejoined her squad. "Maggie, would you please come up here and show the group your school cheer."

Maggie beamed as she ran through her routine. Then Keisha gave each girl a turn to show off her own cheer.

"That was terrific," called Keisha. "You can do some of those moves as we run out onto the field this afternoon. They'll really get the instructors' attention!"

"All riiight!" cried the girls.

"Did you notice that some of your school cheers had moves from today's pom-pon routine in them? You already know the high V, the broken T, and the drop-down inverted V. So let's get that sequence down now."

The girls quickly picked up the routine.

"Hey, everyone," shouted Keisha. "Let's tell the camp who we are."

Give me an "L" - - -"L"

Give me an "I" - - -"I"

Give me an "O" - - -"O"

Give me an "N" - - -"N"

Give me an "S" - - -"S"

What's it spell?

LIONS!

Who's going to be the best today?

LIONS!

Chapter
Seven

POM-PONS
AND PYRAMIDS

Things were finally going well. Keisha didn't realize it was time for lunch until she saw workmen setting up picnic tables at the far end of the stadium. She told Lisa to run ahead and save them a table so that the squad could eat together. It wasn't until she was standing in the food line that Keisha realized she was starving. She helped herself to a sandwich, yogurt, and a banana.

51

Over the next hour the girls really got to relax and know one another.

It turned out that Tina and a girl named Nancy were from the same town but had never met, and the other girls had come from all over the United States. Some had saved money and done fundraising just to get there.

After lunch Keisha and her squad were raring to go. "Now we're going to practice our pyramid for the final session. We've only got a little over an hour to get it right. Do you think we can do it?"

"Yes!" shouted girls as they headed back to their practice area. But most of them looked hesitantly at Keisha.

"Come on, we're the Lions! Which squad has the most spirit?"

"The Lions!"

"And who is going to do their best today?"

"The Lions!"

"That's right. Now the pyramid will need four spotters to make sure we do it safely and correctly." Three girls jumped up right away and volunteered. "We still need one more spotter. Who's it going to be?" Keisha was surprised when Maggie raised her hand. "Yeah, Maggie!" she cheered into her megaphone. "Then, we'll need five of you to be the base," Keisha continued. "Four girls will do cartwheels and then handspring mounts onto the kneeling bases. The spotters will hand poms up to the standing mounters once they're into position. "Who's ready to make our pyramid the best!" she shouted.

"We are!" The reply rang across the field.

Keisha asked everyone to take off their rings, necklaces, bracelets, and earrings and hand them to her. Then she had them wait for instructions while she set the jewelry down and checked her papers. Keisha smiled, "Does any-one need to get rid of chewing gum?" She was glad no one handed her any.

"Okay," Keisha called. "Now the rest of you need to decide who's going to be in the base and who's going to be mounters." She stepped back to let the girls make their choices on their own.

When the girls got into position, Keisha reminded all of them about hands-on spotting as she helped the spotters to make sure they were standing as close as possible to the performers. That way, if anyone started to fall they could catch her right away.

"Okay," cried Keisha. "This time around we are going to get into a line. I want the spotters at the front so that they can run to their places first.

Spotters, do you know where your places are?" The spotters nodded.

"Excellent. Next in line will be the base for the pyramid. Bases, what do you say?" The five girls responded with a big cheer and Keisha smiled.

"Great. Next will come the mounters. Girls, please take your places in line."

The pom-pon routine would lead right into the pyramid, and the girls would have to set their poms aside. Keisha wanted to watch their running style and spacing. So she asked them to run to the wall and back, but to keep their poms with them. The girls took off without hesitation, running in a single line to the field wall and back. The line was a little ragged, but they did just as Keisha had asked.

As the last girl reached her, Keisha called out, "Okay, let's show that Lion spirit now! Are we ready?" she screamed. But it was to get the girls even more excited, not because she was angry with them.

"GO Lions!" the girls shouted, jumping and clapping loudly.

Keisha quickly ran through the arm signals she would use and reminded the girls to keep their eyes on her and move with plenty of spirit. She inspected the row to see if the girls were evenly lined up, waited a few seconds, then raised her arm above her head. With a big smile, she counted to three. "Rev 'em up, Lions. Let's do it," she called as she dropped her arm to her side. One after the other, the girls sprang to their pyramid positions.

"Up we go, Lions!"

Darcy was a little shaky as she climbed onto her base, but with Maggie's spotting she made it with no problem. The pyramid was perfect! The whole squad gave an enormous cheer. After they had carefully dismounted, the girls all ran up to hug Keisha. And she gave each and every one a hug right back.

They practiced a few more times, but it didn't seem to go as well as the first try. Once, two of the mounters missed their marks and the entire base line fell over sideways. The next time, one of the girls in the base was too far from the others. Luckily, Tina caught the problem and had the bases move closer together. Keisha blew her whistle and called time out.

"What do little Lions grow up to be?" she asked while the girls untangled themselves. "Why, they grow up to be mighty Lions! And what do mighty Lions do?"

"They fall on their chins" said Lisa with an embarrassed smile.

"But they roar while they're doing it!" Maggie said.

Keisha's laugh was infectious, and even Lisa joined in. "Okay! And so what are we going to do today?"

"We're going to *roar*," shouted the squad.

"And why?"

"Because we're mighty!"

"We're what?"

"We're Mighty Lions! Hear us ROAR!"

As if on cue, Shannon appeared and announced that it was time to join the other squads for the evaluations. As the group ran to get their poms and join the other girls, she gave Keisha the thumbs-up sign.

When Keisha looked around at the girls in their different colored uniforms, she thought the field actually shimmered. Every girl stood straight and tall as they waited for Shannon to start the activities.

The first squad did handsprings in unison, forming a V-shaped line on the ground as each member came out of the jump. Keisha had to admit she was pretty impressed. When she glanced at her squad, she could see the worried looks on their faces.

Pom-pons and Pyramids

"Don't worry!" cheered Keisha. "We're Lions and we're the best! We've got pride!"

"Deep inside!" the girls shouted and laughed.

Keisha carefully watched each squad perform. Some squads worked in perfect unity, while others seemed unsure of their routines. Keisha was glad she had made her group practice several times. We can do it, she thought. We really can win this. Soon it was the Lions' turn to perform.

The two-level pyramid was one of the hardest stunts for the camp, but the Lions performed it flawlessly!

When it was time for the pom-pon routine, the Lions and the other squads lined up from goalpost to goalpost. Then Keisha joined Shannon and the other group leaders to take their squads through the exercise. When her girls finished their part and took their places alongside the others, Keisha had never felt more proud. At the end of the routine Keisha blew her whistle and signaled her group to follow her.

"The Lions are the best squad here, and nobody can beat you. I think we should all give ourselves a cheer!"

We're the mighty Lions!
We can't be stopped!
We're the mighty Lions!
And we're on top!

Now everyone could see the Lions were really a team and they each received the highest honor—a Blue Superior ribbon. Keisha knew it was time to go. She handed her clipboard and charts to Maggie, told her she was going to the bathroom, and grabbed her pom-pons and megaphone. She turned to the group and spoke through the megaphone. "Thanks to all of you for your hard work—and a special thanks to you, Maggie. You guys really started over and pulled this team together." Then she jogged across the stadium field.

Keisha entered the locker room and stood in front of the mirror. She began to do the squad pom-pon routine, and when she came out of the turn, she found herself in the attic once more.

She was ready to go home. She replaced the uniform, pom-pons, megaphone, and sneakers exactly as she had found them and closed the trunk. As Keisha turned out the overhead light, she snatched up the key.

"Ellie," she called, running down the stairs to search for her friend. Ellie met Keisha at the bottom of the staircase.

"Well?" asked Ellie. "What happened? Come tell me everything."

"Oh, Ellie, it was wonderful! Well at least it ended up being wonderful. The beginning was horrible."

"What did you do? What costume did you choose?"

"I chose the cheerleading costume, Ellie!" said Keisha proudly. "Right away I was picked as one of the squad leaders, and boy did I have a lot to learn!" Suddenly Keisha thought about her friends. "Ellie, would you mind if I came back tomorrow to tell you about my adventure? Right now I've got some explaining to do to Alison, Megan, and Heather."

"Of course I don't mind, Keisha. See your friends."

Keisha ran out of the house, and Ellie's heavy oak door closed softly behind her.

Chapter Eight

KEISHA'S VICTORY

When Keisha bounded through the door, she called her three friends and asked if they could meet at her house after dinner.

Heather was the first to arrive, followed by Alison and Megan a few minutes later. Soon, all four friends were seated side by side on Keisha's bed.

"So, did you go to the attic?" asked Megan.

"I sure did, and I'll bet you'll never guess which costume I chose."

"Cheerleading!" Their voices rang out in unison.

"Yep, and I had the most incredible experience. I ended up in cheerleading camp with about sixty other girls."

"Oh, Keisha, that's perfect for you," said Heather, clapping her hands.

"So what happened?" Alison asked.

"Well, I started my cheer in front of the mirror. I went into a spin, and when I opened my eyes all those girls were facing me."

"Wow! Were you scared?" asked Heather.

"No, not really. I was kind of in shock. Then before I got a chance to even figure out where I was, my name was announced to head up one of the squads."

"You were a squad leader? Magnificent!" Alison gave Keisha a high-five.

"And you were a great cheerleader, right?" Megan was all ears. "Remember what happened to Heather with the junior ballet?"

"Oh yes, I was a great cheerleader. That was part of the problem."

Alison wrinkled her brow. "What do you mean?"

"Well, being good at cheering didn't help me realize that I didn't know how to lead the group. I had a hard time letting other people share in all the things I knew how to do." Alison, Heather, and Megan exchanged glances. "I know just what you guys are thinking. That's why I asked you to meet me here." Keisha smiled at her friends. "I want to apologize about hogging all the time at my party—and tell you about my adventure, of course."

"You don't have to apologize for anything, Keisha," said Heather.

"Oh yes she does!" Alison laughed. "Keisha, sometimes you just get too carried away."

"Well, I realize that now, Ali. I had to learn to let the other girls in my squad have a chance to show that they're good at something. Anyway, I just wanted to say I'm sorry to all of you. I hope you're not mad at me anymore."

"Don't worry, Keish. We could *never* stay mad at you," said Alison, winking at her friend.

Megan turned to Heather and Alison. "What do you think, girls? Should we or shouldn't we?"

Alison was about to answer when Heather interrupted. "Oh, please let me ask her, Megan."

"Well, okay." Megan grinned. "I suppose you may."

Heather bowed to Keisha with a flourish. "Keisha, would you teach us your cheerleading routine?"

"I thought you'd never ask!" Keisha laughed as she leaped off the bed and began her cheer. The girls whooped and clapped as Keisha performed.

A few weeks later, the moment Keisha had been waiting for finally arrived. The band began to play in the gymnasium. Keisha couldn't resist running to the doorway and peeking in. There were so many people in the bleachers that she couldn't spot her parents or see any of her friends in the crowd.

The captain of the squad came and stood behind Keisha. "Are you nervous?" she asked. "I know I am."

"Yes, kind of," said Keisha quietly. "I just hope I remember the routine."

The captain, Carrie, looked at her and smiled. "Oh, we're all going to be great today! And you've got an extra special part to do, Keisha. Just remember to keep your attention on the stunt leader and visualize what you want to do."

"Thanks, Carrie," said Keisha. I hope I'll be as nice as Carrie if I get to be a squad leader again, she thought.

Carrie smiled warmly back at Keisha. "Go out there and break a leg!" she said. Then she turned to the rest of the squad who had gathered behind them. "Okay, it's time to rev 'em up!"

The crowd seemed ready for a great time. They were already shouting and clapping as the squad entered the gym. The applause and cheering grew louder and louder as each cheerleader bounded across the room with an individual set of gymnastic tricks—somersaults, handsprings, cartwheels, roundoffs. By the time the whole squad was in, the gym was rocking with noise. Keisha felt the floor vibrating from all the stomping sneakers in the bleachers.

Carrie whistled twice more, and four kids cartwheeled out and took their positions kneeling as the base. Carrie blew a final blast and the two mounters each did perfect handsprings before the spotters helped them onto the backs of the kids who made up the base. The pyramid was

ready and waiting.

Suddenly every eye turned on Keisha. She just had to do this stunt right!

Taking a deep breath, she broke into a run, gathering momentum. Keisha flew into a handspring, then a stepout, and then straight into a front flip, landing seated in the spotters' arms.

The spotters tossed Keisha into the air again. As she started to come back down, Keisha felt them grab her at the waist to steady her mount onto the top of the pyramid. She rose to her tiptoes and brought her arms up in a victory V. The crowd went wild, and three cries of "Hip, Hip, Hooray!" resounded through the gym. The applause was like thunder.

They had done it! Keisha's dream had come true!

Diary

Dear Diary,

Hi, it's Keisha. I had an incredible day today! This was the first time our cheerleading squad got to perform at a game. All our practicing was really worth doing . . . We were terrific! And the team played a great game, too.

I still think about the day Ms. Henderson announced that I made the squad. When she called my name, I felt a shiver go right through me! The squad met after school, and Ms. H. gave everyone a cheerleader poster. Alison, Megan, and Heather congratulated me right away. They told me how proud they were of me and that they knew I could do it. Then Heather said that the minute I told them about my adventure in the attic, she was sure I would make the squad.

I wonder how Maggie and Shannon and the Lions did the rest of the week, and whether any of our squad made it to the free choreography training. I'll always remember how great it felt when everybody worked together. I sure won't give my squad leader a hard time!

My poster is still up right in the middle of my bulletin board so I can see it the first thing in the morning and the last thing at night. Funny, but the poster also makes me think of Ellie's attic and how nice it is to share your dreams.

Good night Diary,

Keisha

JOIN THE MAGIC ATTIC CLUB!

You can enjoy every adventure of the Magic Attic Club just by reading all the books. And there's more!

You can have a whole world of fun with the dolls, outfits, and accessories that are based on the books. And since Alison, Keisha, Heather, and Megan can wear one another's clothes, you can relive their adventures, or create new ones of your own!

To join the Magic Attic Club, just fill out this postcard and drop it in the mail, or call toll free **1-800-221-6972**. We'll send you a **free** membership kit

including a poster, bookmark, postcards, and a catalog with all four dolls.

With your first purchase of a doll, you'll also receive your own key to the attic. And it's FREE!

Yes, I want to join the Magic Attic Club!

My name is _____

My address is _____

City _____ State_____ Zip _____

Birth date _____ Parent's signature _____

11901

And send a catalog to my friend, too!

Her name is _____

Her address is_____

City _____ State_____ Zip _____

11902

If someone has already used the postcard from this book and you would like a free Magic Attic Club catalog, just send your full name and address to:

Magic Attic Club
866 Spring Street
P.O. Box 9712
Portland, ME 04104-9954

Or call toll free
1-800-221-6972

Code: 11906

BUSINESS REPLY MAIL

FIRST-CLASS MAIL PERMIT NO. 8905 PORTLAND ME

POSTAGE WILL BE PAID BY THE ADDRESSEE

MAGIC ATTIC CLUB
866 SPRING ST
PO BOX 9712
PORTLAND ME 04104-9954